JOHNNY APPLESEED

A Tale of Love

Adapted by Jennifer Boudart

Illustrated by Rusty Fletcher

PUBLICATIONS INTERNATIONAL, LTD.

There once was a traveler named Johnny Appleseed. He was born in Boston, Massachusetts, around 1775. When Johnny was 26 years old, he set out to travel across America. He had collected apple seeds in the East and then carried them in a sack slung over his shoulder. As he traveled, Johnny spread the seeds across the land. When settlers came from the East, they found Johnny's apple orchards and felt right at home.

Not all the seeds ended up as trees in an orchard, though. Sometimes they fell by the side of the road and started to grow. This is a story about one of those seeds.

This seed fell from Johnny's pack as he walked away from a village where a few settlers lived. A little stream ran just outside the village. The seed landed beside this stream.

As luck would have it, the soil there was very good for growing trees. It wasn't long before a tender sapling shot up out of the ground. Soon after, the sapling started to look like a tree. Then the sapling sprouted a crown of branches tipped with emerald green leaves. With each passing day, the tree seemed to grow a little bit stronger. Johnny would have liked the way this new tree was growing.

Years passed, and the young sapling grew into a fine tree. Each spring, more settlers passed by as they headed west. The small path became more worn into the ground from the wagons and people passing by.

Each year the tree welcomed the newest additions to the deer and rabbit families. The tree's branches filled with quick-footed squirrels. A bird family built a nest in the branches, and its bark was home to beetles and caterpillars.

Each fall the tree's summer friends headed south or hibernated for winter. Then its leaves dropped to the ground, and it settled down for a winter's nap.

More time passed, and the settler's village became a town. The tree stood high above the well-worn path, which was now covered with cement.

Now the town was busy. It was filled with houses, factories, and people. The tree heard a lot more than singing birds and gurgling water from the stream. The town noises mixed in with the other sounds that the tree had always known. Many people chose the big tree as a favorite place for picnics.

Unfortunately, with all the people and noise, the deer and rabbits were scared away. The tree missed them, but at least some animals still came to visit.

One day a loud rumbling noise woke the tree. A big machine came and started digging holes in the ground. The tree heard the workers say that the town was "booming." The tree wasn't quite sure what that meant.

Soon tall buildings were built and the town became a city. The buildings blocked the sunlight. The smoke from the factories made the tree choke and even turned some of its leaves yellow. Cement sidewalks replaced the stream and crowded the tree. Soon all that was left was a tiny patch of grass around the tree's trunk. Perhaps worst of all, the people were too busy to notice the tree.

Then one day a family moved into an apartment building across the street from the tree. The family had a little boy who was sad because he didn't know anyone he could play with.

When his mom went to the store, the boy asked for her permission to play outside. He would run up to the tree and wrap his arms around the massive trunk. Then he'd climb up the trunk just as fast as a squirrel! The happy tree would hold its branches out strong and still so the boy wouldn't slip. Sometimes the boy would pretend he was a cowboy riding through the hills in the distance. The tree was the boy's favorite place.

One afternoon the boy's mother called him to come inside. But he was asleep in the tree. His mother was worried so she asked some neighbors to help look for him. They were calling for the boy when someone looked up and saw the sleeping boy in the apple tree's branches. They called to him.

The sleepy boy opened his eyes and saw the crowd below. "Come down! You'll get hurt!" called his mother.

"Don't worry," answered the boy. "This tree is my friend."

An old man chuckled. "It's true," he said. "I napped in this tree when I was a boy." Then everyone remembered the tree from when they were young.

Everyone felt very sad because of what they had let happen to the tree. "This tree has been a friend to all of us. We should give it a better home!" the boy said.

"Let's build a park," said someone in the crowd.

"Yes!" the people cheered.

In just a few days, there was a loud rumbling sound again! With the help of the big machines, the people were able to move the tree to a small park.

A neighborhood store owner sent over some benches and swings. Soon birds filled the trees and made the tree very happy!

As if by magic, the park seemed to change life around the neighborhood. The people made time for picnics and playing. Children climbed in the tree branches. Birds and animals visited the trees and nibbled on the apples.

The little boy continued to visit the tree, even when he was a grown man with a family of his own. He would sit in the grass and lean against his old friend's trunk. When he did, the old tree's leaves would rustle and dance, even on the calmest days.

As a boy, he reminded the busy townspeople that every living thing needs love.

One to Grow On
Love

In this story, we see the difference love makes to the tree, the boy, and the other people in the city. We also see that when a group of people work together, they can make good things happen. When you're outdoors, pay attention to the world around you. Take time to plant a tree or feed the birds with a friend. It's an act of love that everyone will appreciate!